FAGIN'S GIRL

KAREN McCOMBIE

Illustrated by
Anneli Bray

First published in 2022 in Great Britain by
Barrington Stoke Ltd
18 Walker Street, Edinburgh, EH3 7LP

www.barringtonstoke.co.uk

Text © 2022 Karen McCombie
Illustrations © 2022 Anneli Bray

A CIP catalogue record for this book is available
from the British Library upon request

ISBN: 978-1-80090-055-4

Printed by Hussar Books, Poland

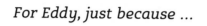

For Eddy, just because ...

CONTENTS

PART 1: London, 1836

PART 2: Australia, 1988

PART *1*

London
1836

CHAPTER 1

A lucky day indeed ...

I stretched out in the bed, yawning as I woke up. My two long braids of hair spread out over the white pillow. Then I remembered what day it was and sat up fast.

There was Mother at the table, already at work with piles of fabric and scissors and thin strands of wire. The morning light streamed in the window behind her. It made her red hair glow like the embers of our tiny fire on a cold evening.

"Good morning, Ettie!" Mother called over to me. "And birthday greetings to you, my dear! Ten years old today ... what a grown girl you are!"

Mother's smile was as bright as the sun. No matter how bad things got, her smile made everything better.

"You should have woken me up!" I said as I swung my legs out of the creaky metal bed I

shared with Mother. I looked down to check if my brother Joe's mattress was on the floor still, but it had already been pushed away under the bed. Joe was older than me by two years. He never called me Ettie – always Bean, because I was as small as a bean to him no matter how old I got.

The floor was cold to my bare feet, so I jumped onto the rag rug. Then I hurried behind the curtain in the corner where our clothes hung neatly from wooden pegs on the wall.

"Well, today you deserve to have an extra hour in bed, Ettie," said Mother.

I could hear the snip-snip of her scissors as she cut out the flowers and leaves from the fabric we had been given. Every week a box of cloth and wire arrived, and every week Mother and I worked twelve hours or more every day. We made sprays of purple violets, blue forget-me-nots and white honeysuckle for the bonnets of rich ladies.

I always put the flowers together, fitting them on the strips of wire. Mother made the leaves, dusting them with a powder that gave them a vivid green shine and slipping them on last.

"Has Joe left for work already?" I asked Mother as I changed out of my night things and pulled on my dress and petticoat. I wasn't sure what time it was. Maybe seven o'clock? We all got up before six normally.

We'd have our breakfast of bread and butter and milk too, if we had any. Then Joe would hurry off to the brewery. It was his job to clean out the stables there once the horses were harnessed to the carts and they'd set off to deliver barrels of beer to the pubs of London.

"Joe is just fetching the water for us, then he'll be away," said Mother.

The door banged, and Joe was back.

I pulled the curtain to one side and grinned at my brother. But Joe looked sad. Or angry maybe. Or as if he had a secret that was bothering him.

Joe talked to me less and less these days. If he did have a secret, I didn't think he was going to tell me ...

CHAPTER 2

Joe's secret

"There were so many people at the standpipe getting water this morning," Joe grumbled. He set down the bucket with a clatter, spilling some of the water. Joe was clumsy. If there was a stone to trip over, he'd trip. If there was a plate to drop, he'd drop it.

"And what do you say to your sister on this lucky day?" Mother said to Joe.

Joe frowned as he took off his jacket.

"I don't know why you always call birthdays 'lucky', Mother!" Joe snapped at her.

Mother kept calm. Ever since Father died, Joe found it hard to see the good in things.

"Joe, we must always count our blessings," Mother said. "And on birthdays, we should always remember how lucky we are to be here. Remember, there are so many little angels that never had the chance to grow up."

Mother was talking about the sadness that nearly every family knew. It didn't matter if you were rich or poor, illness could come to babies and young ones that were not yet strong. In our own family, Ada and Will and Lily were born before me and Joe. But they'd all been buried before we'd even arrived in this world.

"Well, I don't feel lucky to be here, in this room," said Joe, sweeping his hand around.

When Father had been alive, we'd had two rooms and a scullery for our kitchen things. It was a very cosy home, with many comforts.

9

Father's job as a clerk had meant we could afford for me and Joe to go to the church school. We'd come home to wonderful smells as Mother cooked dinner on our very own stove.

But then poor Father's heart had given out and things changed fast. Me and Joe had to leave school and get work instead. We left behind our nice home and now lived in just one room in a house packed with other families.

We shared a toilet in the yard that was never very clean. We had no stove to cook on, so we had to buy our food from the handcarts that went up and down the road. Most of the time we could only afford bread, but now and again Mother saved up for a meat pie or a kipper that we'd all share.

"I know it's hard, Joe," Mother said in the steady way she always spoke. "But we are truly lucky to have this home when so many poor souls are in the workhouse or sleeping in the street."

Joe said nothing to that. But then he took
something from his pocket and handed it to me.

"For you, Bean," Joe mumbled.

My brother hadn't forgotten my birthday!
I opened the small paper package and found

a biscuit. It was sprinkled with sugar and smelled of honey and cinnamon. It looked so delicious!

"Oh, thank you!" I said, going over to Joe and planting a kiss on his cheek.

He pretended to be disgusted. But I knew he was pleased to see how happy I was.

"How kind of you, Joe!" said Mother. "How did you afford it?"

Joe didn't earn much. And he gave all his money to Mother on pay-day. We couldn't have managed the rent without it.

"I got a bit extra from Mr Blake last week for doing a good job," said Joe. He sounded cross with Mother for asking.

"Oh, the stable boss is so kind!" said Mother with her sunshine smile. "Now you'd better be off, Joe. You don't want to be late and lose your job."

Joe suddenly looked strange. His jaw was tight and his lips were twitching. It was as if words were trying to burst out of his mouth and he was struggling to hold them back.

But out they tumbled.

"Mr Blake is NOT a good man!" Joe yelled. "Would a good man do this?"

Joe turned his back to us and pulled up his shirt.

His skinny back was covered with blue and yellow bruises.

"Joe!" Mother gasped. "Mr Blake did this to you?"

"Yes – for spilling horse feed on the ground," said Joe, turning to face us again. "He beat me, then told me to go. He said he'd find a more careful boy to do my job."

I thought of the colour of the bruises. They were old. Joe had not been hit just yesterday.

"When did this happen?" I asked.

"A week ago," Joe said, and tucked his shirt back in.

"But where have you been going every day?" Mother asked with alarm in her voice. "And you gave me money on Friday – where did that come from?"

"You don't need to know," said Joe. He put his chin up as if daring her to ask more.

"Are you doing something that could get you into trouble?" said Mother. "Please, please don't do that, Joe! You can work with Ettie and me. We can ask to make more flowers if there's three of us ..."

"I'm not doing the work of women and girls!" Joe shouted. "Not when I can make better money!"

"Joe – no! I forbid it!" said Mother, banging her fist on the table.

I jumped. I had never seen Mother lose her temper like that.

Joe said nothing. He grabbed his jacket and shoved it on.

"Joe! Where are you going?" Mother demanded.

But Joe left, slamming the door behind him. Just like that, my brother was gone.

I had no idea that I wouldn't see him again for five long months – and that my life till then would not feel lucky at all ...

CHAPTER 3

Ettie all alone

It was May when Joe left.

In June Mother and I moved to a smaller and cheaper room in a run-down house along the road. There was space for a bed and two stools and not much else. But Mother made it as nice as she could by pinning a pretty patterned shawl over the window at night and putting a posey of fake flowers in an old jam jar on the shelf.

In July Mother's cough started, and her hands became covered in bleeding sores.

In August Mother took to her bed, still trying to make the bonnet flowers with me whenever she had the energy.

In September Mother died. She was buried in a pauper's grave, with only me and a neighbour to say goodbye.

"How will you manage, Ettie?" Mrs Price asked as we stood by Mother's grave. "Have you family who could take you in?" She lived in the room next door to ours. It was the same size as ours, with her, Mr Price and two young children in it.

"I have no family that I know of," I said. Father had a brother I'd met when I was young, but he had gone away to America to start a new life. I didn't know where my uncle might be in that huge country.

"You have a brother, you told me?" said Mrs Price as we set off from the churchyard.

"I have, but I don't know where Joe is," I said as I dabbed at my eyes with the hem of my sleeve. I had spent the last few months looking around every corner, wondering if Joe was near or far, alive or dead.

"But how will you manage, Ettie?" asked Mrs Price again. "A child cannot live alone. Will you see if the workhouse will take you in?"

The workhouse! Everyone feared it. It was where families were split up, worked half to death and fed badly.

"No!" I said fast. "I have paid the rent till Monday. And I'll work harder on the flowers, you'll see!"

Mrs Price smiled at me, but her eyes were full of worry. She wondered what would become of me – a ten-year-old girl alone in the world.

As we walked along the dusty road, I wondered and worried too.

CHAPTER 4

Becoming a nobody

I was woken at dawn by the sound of birdsong –
and the hedgehog snuffling round my hand,
seeking out the crumbs of the bread I'd eaten
before I'd fallen asleep.

It took me a minute to think what day it
was and where I was.

And then I remembered – Mother was
buried just last week and today was Monday.
The day the rent man would come for his
money. But I had none to give him, so I had
slipped away yesterday evening.

I'd tiptoed down the creaky stairs of
the house with a sack. It was filled with

some underclothes, a hairbrush, a candle and matches, my other dress, a blanket and Mother's thick wool shawl.

I had sold Mother's pretty patterned shawl the day before. There were a few other things I'd sold to a man in the market: plates and spoons, a small mirror, a brooch and hairpin of Mother's. They'd earned me a few pennies.

As for where I was ... it was the same churchyard where Mother was buried. Yesterday I'd found a corner where the bushes were thick and covered by a roof of tree branches. I'd crawled underneath and found a dry spot where I could hide away. I'd wrapped the blanket around me and used the sack of clothes as my pillow.

And now I sat up, shaking my aching bones.

Life in the city started early, and I needed to be ready for it. I had taken one more thing from our room before I left, and it would earn me my living: a wooden broom. I took hold of it from beside the sack. Today I would seek out the busiest roads nearby and become a street-sweeper!

I had seen other boys and girls do it. They'd stand on a busy road where horses and carriages rattled and clopped by. A fine lady or gent would look this way and that, ready to cross. That was when a street-sweeper would leap in front of them, swooshing their broom from side to side to sweep away the dust, mud and horse muck. Then the ladies could step on the cobblestones without dirtying their long dresses, and the rich men's shiny shoes could stay shiny.

The grateful men and women would have a coin in their gloved hands, ready to give to the street-sweeper once safe on the other side. I was fast; I was polite. Surely I could earn plenty of money in a day? Maybe more than I ever did twisting cloth into flowers?

That was what I hoped. But by noon I was tired and hungry and had earned nothing. The life of a street-sweeper was much harder than I had thought it to be.

"Please, madam, can I clear your path?" I asked yet another woman who was walking with her maid-servant.

So far I had been ignored or told to go away by everyone I had spoken to. For the first time, this woman looked at me and nodded.

My heart leapt. Perhaps it was the start of my luck changing. The lady was well-off – it was clear from the good dress she wore. Her bonnet was decorated with silk ribbons and roses. Her maid's basket was full of packages. Might she give me a farthing? That was only a quarter of a penny. Might she give me more? A halfpenny? A whole penny?

I smiled and did a curtsey, then stepped out into the road as soon as the traffic calmed

down. Swish, swish went my broom, as fast as
I could swing it. Behind me I heard the rustle
of the lady's wide skirts and the clip-clip of her
heeled shoes on the cobbles.

I got to the other side and turned, holding my hand out.

But the lady just walked by me, like a great sailing ship passing a little rowing boat.

"Please, madam! Can't you spare anything at all?" I begged.

The lady strode on, her maid trailing after her. They were both deaf to my pleading.

I held tight to the broom and cried where I stood. No one seemed to notice. I had become a nobody. Like a ghost child.

I had always tried to count my blessings as Mother did. But I could see no blessings and no luck about me today.

Till I heard my name spoken.

"Bean – is it you?" said my brother Joe.

CHAPTER 5

Together again

Joe and I sat together on the steps of the church.

I felt full of joy at finding my brother again. And at eating the hot piece of pie he shared with me!

And Joe was very glad to have found me. But he was heartbroken to learn that Mother was gone and I had been left all alone.

"I am so sorry that I went away," said Joe as he wrapped his arm around me. "I thought Mother was angry with me. I decided I'd earn lots of money and come back and surprise her with it."

"And have you earned lots of money?" I asked.

"I haven't got as much money as I'd like yet," Joe said with a shrug. "But Mr Fagin says I'm a good boy and will do well if I work hard."

"Who is Mr Fagin?" I asked. "And what work do you do for him?"

Joe didn't answer at first. But after a moment he said, "Mr Fagin deals in second-hand things. Me and some other boys find items for him and he sells them on. He gives us a place to stay too."

I thought of the man in the market who bought Mother's bits and pieces from me. There were plenty of shops and stalls selling goods that had been owned and used by many people before. Only rich people bought brand-new things.

So it seemed Joe had a good job. I was about to ask more about his work when he spoke.

"I don't know what to do, Bean," said Joe. "I can't leave you here ..."

"Maybe I can work for Mr Fagin as well?" I asked. "I'm quick to learn. I could find things like you. Or I'm good at sewing and mending and making – I could do that. Couldn't I, Joe?"

"Yes, Bean," said Joe. "But I don't know if Mr Fagin wants another worker. And if he does ... well, you're a girl. He only has boys working for him."

Joe scratched at his head and stared down at his scuffed boots.

I had an idea.

"Look, Joe!" I said, and rolled up my skirt. "I took these with me to keep warm."

Under my skirt and petticoat I was wearing a pair of patched breeches that Joe had left behind.

Joe laughed at the sight of a girl in boy's clothing. Next I stole the hat off his head, as quick as a wink. I bundled my two long braids up into the hat and grinned at him.

"Well?" I said. "I look like you now, don't I? I can pass as your little brother!"

"Never!" said Joe.

But then he looked at me. Properly looked.

"Wait here, Bean," Joe called out as he stood up and hurried off down the steps. "Don't go anywhere!"

Of course I'd wait for him. I had nowhere else to go ...

CHAPTER 6

Lost and found

Joe was gone an hour. It was an hour that felt like for ever. I worried he'd vanished on me again.

"Here, Bean!" Joe called out as he threw a bundle of things at me.

"Where did you get them?" I asked.

From the bundle, I held up a torn and patched white shirt and a small waistcoat. Joe pulled a cloth cap out of his pocket and put it on my head, taking back his hat, which I'd still been wearing.

"Borrowed them, didn't I?" said Joe. "Anyway, I've got good news! I spoke to Mr Fagin, and he says you can come work for him."

"And stay with you?" I asked.

"And stay with me," Joe said, nodding. "It's only a corner of a room, and the mattress is just hay stuffed in some old sacks."

"I don't care!" I said. "As long as I'm with you, Joe, I'll be fine! What work does Mr Fagin have for me?"

"You're to clean and repair the stuff that me and the other boys find," said Joe. "It's not an easy life at Mr Fagin's. But we can make money and then get our own lodgings one day, Bean."

It had seemed like I'd hit the bottom, but now it felt like I was on my way up again!

And so I hurried to the bushes where I'd made my den. I crawled in as a girl and crawled back out as a boy. Joe took my sack of belongings and off we went.

We walked through busy streets and winding roads. Down one alley, Joe stopped at a stall piled with rags and sold all my girlish things, even my hairbrush. All he kept was the candle and matches and the blanket.

"But how will I brush my hair?" I asked Joe. He was walking fast and I had to hurry to keep up.

"You can't give away any clues that you're a girl, Bean!" Joe said sharply. "Forget your hair. You'll wear your cap all the time."

"All right, Joe," I said.

We were crossing a road now, heading for an old warehouse with broken windows.

"This is it," said Joe. He started to climb up some open wooden steps that clung to the side of the building and led up to the top floor. "Always watch where you put your feet. Some

of the wood is rotten and you could fall straight down if you're not careful!"

And there was a broken step now. It was snapped in half with a view to the ground far below. I hoped no poor boy had fallen down there ...

After a short but careful climb, we were at the top and Joe pushed at a stiff door. It opened into a wide space that smelled of fire smoke and damp walls. Many sacks and rags lay dotted around, where Joe's friends must sleep at night. Above these home-made mattresses were zig-zags of rope strung from wall to wall. Cotton and silk handkerchiefs hung over them. Plain and patterned scarves, and gentlemen's cravats too.

I noticed a fire crackling in a grate. Beside it was a high-backed chair where a man sat. A young boy was on a stool beside him, busy at work with something.

"Ah, Joe, now this must be your brother!" said the man in the chair. He beckoned me over.

"This is Mr Fagin," said Joe as he put his hand on my back and nudged me forward.

"Welcome, Bean," said Mr Fagin, looking me up and down.

"Thank you, sir," I replied. I almost did a curtsey, till I remembered I was a boy!

Mr Fagin scared me. He was as skinny as a wolfhound, with a beard as furry and wiry as that kind of dog. He peered hard at me from behind his round spectacles. Maybe I was scared that Mr Fagin could see me for what I really was – a girl dressed in boys' clothes, her hair stuffed into a cap.

"And I hope you will work as hard as your brother," said Mr Fagin. He was smiling, but his eyes were hard and steely. This made his words sound more like a warning than a wish.

"Yes, sir," I said again. "Please, sir, I can mend and sew things very well. I worked with my mother making decorations for ladies' bonnets."

"Good! We have need of your skills then," Mr Fagin said with a satisfied nod. "The boys I have are experts at finding things on the street, but they are no good at fixing up any dirty or damaged items."

Mr Fagin swept his hands up towards the stuff on the washing lines, then over to some wooden crates on the floor full of leather and lace gloves. Chunky round fob watches were piled up on the mantelpiece of the fire.

"There is a wash-house on the roof, Bean," said Mr Fagin. "Your job is to work there, cleaning and pressing the items brought in

by the lads. Mend them too if it needs doing.
Understand?"

"Yes, sir," I said.

"Joe will show you around," said Mr Fagin. "Then he'll be out for the day – at work like the other boys. If you need anything, you can ask Mouse here."

The young boy on the stool looked up at me shyly. He was about six years old. He really did look like a mouse. I saw that he was busy polishing a gold-topped walking cane. Was that *real* gold? I wondered. How had someone managed to lose that?

"Come on up to the roof," said Joe, and he led the way towards a door on the far wall. "Up there you can see all the way to St Paul's Cathedral!"

"Hold on!" said Mr Fagin. "Here's something for you, Joe. Payment for the present you brought me ..."

He sent a silver fob watch arcing into the air, its chain flying behind it. Joe caught it neatly.

"Thanks, Mr Fagin!" he said with wonder in his face and voice.

And then Joe turned and I followed him. A minute later we were up on the flat roof, with chimneys around us and blue sky above.

"The small building is the wash-house," said Joe. "There's wood inside for a fire, and some buckets to bring up water to heat. The standpipe is at the end of the street. You can hang laundry here, or downstairs if it rains. Mouse can show you where the mending things are kept."

While Joe pointed and explained, I looked at the watch that now peeked from his waistcoat pocket. It looked dented and had a cracked glass front but was still an expensive thing for a boy to have.

"Joe, what present did you bring to Mr Fagin to earn such a thing?" I asked as I pointed to the watch.

"Why, *you*, Bean!" Joe laughed.

I didn't laugh back. It felt as if I had been sold. Just like some broken item that might be worth a shilling or two ...

CHAPTER 7

A close call

After three days I had found my feet at
Mr Fagin's place.

I knew all five of the boys that worked
alongside Joe. Silas was fifteen and unfriendly.
Georgie and Edwin were twins of ten years old,
but they were small and skinny and looked
younger. Cuffy had dark skin and came from
an island very far away, he said. He didn't
know how old he was. He had been a cabin boy
on a ship but was treated badly. He'd escaped
when the ship came into the docks nearby.

And then there was Mouse. In the three
days I'd been there, he hadn't said a thing
to me. "Does Mouse ever speak?" I asked

Joe while I pegged washing up to dry in the fluttering wind.

Joe sat perched on a chimney. "None of us have ever heard him say a word," Joe said. "Not even a squeak. Silas named him Mouse as he was so quiet."

"Hey, Bean," Cuffy's voice interrupted. "I found this today. Got a tear in it. Need you to fix it up!"

Cuffy stood in the doorway to the roof and tossed something at me. It was long and thin, with a wooden handle and black fabric bunched around it.

"An umbrella. Should make Mr Fagin a nice bit of money," Joe said to Cuffy. But Cuffy was already gone. In his place was little Mouse, who was lugging a heavy bucket of water for me.

"It's not an umbrella," I said as I pushed it open. "It's a lady's parasol. It keeps the sun from their faces instead of the rain from their heads."

Parasols were smaller than umbrellas and decorated with lace. I studied the inside of it. It was made so cleverly – tiny stitches held the stiff linen to thin strips of wood.

I spun the handle, twirling the parasol around. I heard a small laugh. It came from Mouse! He stood watching the spinning parasol as if it was as pretty as a firework!

It made me bold to hear Mouse make such a happy noise.

"Watch this!" I called out, and climbed onto one of the large chimney pots. With a whoop and a wave of the parasol, I jumped to the next chimney pot.

I expected more laughs, but instead I heard a gasp.

"Bean – your cap!" Joe called out.

I put my hand up to the hat. And then I felt it – one of my braids had fallen out. I shoved it

back in quickly. Mouse was placing the heavy bucket on the ground. Had he seen anything?

Would he tell Mr Fagin if he did? Mouse might not have the words, but he could pull off my cap in front of the other lads and Mr Fagin if he wanted to ...

I needed to do something fast. And I thought of one of the shops I had seen on the way here that first day.

With my plan, I would make myself safe and earn some money at the same time!

CHAPTER 8

A snip and a chop!

Mr Fagin was nowhere to be seen when I left the warehouse.

In the streets outside, I took a wrong turn or two as I tried to find my way, passing so many things for sale.

There were penny pie shops selling meat puddings and eel pies. Shops that sold caged birds that would brighten a shabby room with their songs, and sparrows with string on their legs for children to play with.

Stalls sold teapots, hot coffee to drink, rat poison, pea soup and old top hats that were frayed and worn but still smart.

Handcarts were heaped with slices of pineapple, bundles of asparagus and watercress, and even small squares of turf for the bottoms of bird cages.

And then there was the entertainment on many of the street corners. A German band played their lively music. An Italian woman sang opera. A man turned the handle of his organ and the tiny monkey chained on top of it danced for the delighted crowds.

But I had little time to stop and listen to any of them. I hurried this way and that till I found the alley and the shop I was looking for.

"What do you want, boy?" asked the woman leaning on the door.

I pulled my cap off, showing her my long braids that reached nearly down to my waist. "How much for this, madam?" I asked, holding up one of my braids.

The woman looked surprised to see that this "boy" was in fact a girl. But then she took the braid and undid the ribbon that held it. She fanned out the hair in her hand. It was brick red, just like Mother's had been. The woman put one hand in the pocket of her apron and drew out some coins.

"I'll give you this," she said, dropping a few into my hand.

The next second, she pulled a great long pair of scissors from her apron pocket. With a tug, a snip and a chop, both my braids were off. The next time I might see them was in a fancy hairpiece a rich lady wore as she rode by in her carriage.

I ran all the way back to the warehouse, stopping only once to buy some black thread with the money I'd earned.

I scrambled up the endless wooden stairs and in the door, coming face to face with Mr Fagin.

"Where have you been, my little Bean?" he asked.

Mr Fagin had that strange smile on his face, like the upturned mouth of a crocodile that was just about to eat you up. Mouse sat on the stool beside him.

"Buying something to mend a parasol, sir,"
I said as I held out the wrap of black thread.

I knew Mr Fagin was my master now, and
that like all masters he wouldn't let me leave
my work without a very good excuse.

I took off my cap to show respect. And to
show Mouse that I had the short-cropped hair
of a boy!

"Very good," Mr Fagin said. "Here ... for the thread and your quick thinking." He handed me a halfpenny. His smile seemed warmer now that I seemed to be a keen worker. "But before you fix up the parasol, I need you for other work today."

"No, sir!" I heard Joe say from a dark corner. "I can manage alone!"

And then I saw that my brother was bent over the mattress that Edwin slept on. Joe was binding a dirty rag around Edwin's arm, along with a long stick.

"You cannot manage your trick alone, Joe!" Mr Fagin barked at him. Then he turned to me with his crocodile smile again. "Bean, Edwin had a fall and may have broken his arm. Joe needs a helper for his work this afternoon."

"But I can take Mouse, sir!" said Joe, coming over to Mr Fagin.

"Are you forgetting something, Joe?" said Mr Fagin as he stared hard at my brother. "For your trick you need a young 'un that can talk!"

Joe had that dark look about him again, like he had a secret he didn't want me to know.

But it didn't seem as if he had a choice.

Mr Fagin had made his decision.

And now I would learn what this "trick" was about ...

CHAPTER 9

Joe's trick

Me and Joe had walked two miles, to the West End of London. I should have been excited to see such fine buildings and grand shops. But I was not, for we had come to do Joe's "trick" and he'd just explained it to me.

It was basically stealing.

My heart was ripped in two …

"I can't believe you lied to me," I sobbed. I used Mother's hankie to dab at my eyes. "You said you and the other boys found lost things. But you don't. You're pickpockets and thieves!"

"I didn't want you to know, Bean!" said Joe as he pushed me forward along the pavement. "Look – I hoped we'd earn the money to leave and get a place of our own soon. Then I could get work at another stable, like I did before. You could make your flowers again. We'd be all right."

We scurried along and well-off folk stared at us as if we were dirt. They shooed us away with their gloved hands or canes.

"We aren't going to be all right if we're caught robbing, Joe!" I cried.

"We'll be fine," said Joe. "Just do what I say and we could get something really good. Make some proper money and get away from Fagin for ever."

I didn't see how that could happen. If Joe was a good earner for Mr Fagin, he'd never let Joe leave. And that made me think of the other poor boys in Mr Fagin's gang. Young lads with nowhere else to go. They took all the risk while Fagin took most of the money. Joe had told me that Edwin had broken his arm when he'd tried to dip his hand in a gentleman's pocket and been pushed away into the road. Edwin's arm went straight under the hoof of a horse.

But broken bones weren't the worst of it. Those caught stealing would be put in prison for years. Or they might get sent on a ship to Australia – transported away to a life of working without rest in a far, far away country, never to see their loved ones again.

I was frightened. I cried till I knew I must look a dreadful sight. My eyes stung from the tears.

"Trust me, it'll be quick and easy, Bean!" Joe tried to tell me. "And you crying like that is good! People will pity you and not see what I'm up to ..."

Joe's trick was this – he'd choose a rich person and I was to try to beg from them. While I distracted them, Joe would steal their watch or wallet or purse. With the job done, we'd hurry away in different directions and meet up a street or two away.

"Here – now! Him!" Joe hissed.

We were next to a shop with its name written in gold lettering: "James Smith & Sons". The huge plate-glass windows were packed with all sorts of umbrellas, parasols and canes. A gentleman in a top hat holding a silver-topped cane had just stepped out of the door.

I didn't know what else to do but follow my brother's orders.

After all, Joe only wanted the best for me. For us to be together.

I had a heavy heart and tears streaming down my cheeks as I stepped in front of the man.

"Please, sir, I'm lost!" I said.

"So? What's that got to do with me?" he said gruffly.

"I'm all alone!" I said. "Can you spare me a coin for a bit of food till I find my way home?"

Out of the corner of my eye I saw Joe slip his hand into the gentleman's pocket and gently pull something out.

"Get out of my way!" the man ordered. He stepped to the left to go around me. But I made the mistake of stepping to that side too. Then we both did it again. This silly dance might have been funny if it was done with a friend. But it made the rich man furious.

"OUT OF MY WAY, BOY!" he roared, and lifted his cane.

The man was about to strike me. The end of his cane had a heavy silver eagle's head on it. If the eagle's beak hit my skull, it would split it open.

I curled up in a ball and felt the red-hot pain of it burn my back instead. Again and again and again. And then everything became a jumble of hurt and noise and shouting.

"No! Leave her alone!" I heard Joe call out.

"Get this creature off my back!" the man yelped.

I heard feet pounding from all directions. Raised voices. Joe yelling. The man cried out, "The wretch robbed me! They BOTH robbed me!"

"Not her – she's just a beggar!" shouted Joe. "I don't know her! It was me that robbed him. Just me!"

"Is it a girl?" I heard someone ask. "These are boy's clothes!"

"My name is Ettie," I gasped as the pain stung my back.

"She *is* a little girl!" said a woman's voice.

I felt arms around me, lifting me up. But they were gentle – not like the arms I now saw were gripping Joe tight.

"Little girl – do you know this boy?" a stranger asked me, pointing his arm at Joe.

My brother's eyes were pleading. He was silently begging me to say something that would mean I'd not see him for a long time. Or for ever.

I did what my big brother wanted me to do.

"No! I don't know him!" I said.

The gentle arms led me away into the cool and calm of the umbrella shop.

The last sight I had of my brother was of him being dragged backwards along the pavement by an angry crowd of men ...

Ettie and Joe Shaw. Loving sister and brother. What would Mother say if she knew our luck was lost?

PART 2

Australia
1988

CHAPTER 10

Then and now

Lauren tapped her foot nervously under the school desk. It would be her turn to get up and talk soon.

She looked at the banner pinned up at the front of the class: *"Celebrating Australia's Bicentennial 1788–1988!"*

All over Australia there were big events happening this year – 1988. Especially here in Sydney, because it was where the First Fleet of eleven convict ships arrived from England two hundred years ago.

Lauren's teacher, Miss Jenner, had set the students a project to mark the celebrations.

They each had to recite a speech in front of the class about what made Australia great.

Lauren's friend Kenny went first. He spoke about all the animals that were native to Australia. Animals they didn't have anywhere else in the world, like kangaroos and koalas and dingos. Kenny was really nervous about his speech but did OK till he tried to say "duck-billed platypus". He said "buck-dilled flatty-puss" instead and everyone burst out laughing.

It was Bindi's turn after that. No one laughed when Bindi spoke because she was kind of angry. She said it was ridiculous to say Australia "began" when a bunch of prisoners set foot in the country after being sent here on a boat. Aboriginal people had been in Australia for thousands and thousands of years by that time.

Lauren liked Bindi a lot, and she knew it was hard for Bindi's family being Aboriginal

Australians when everyone was going on
and on about the anniversary of the English
arriving.

But it made Lauren nervous about doing her
own presentation ...

"Lauren?" said Miss Jenner. "Come on up!"

Lauren gulped. She grabbed a piece of paper from her desk and shuffled up to the front of the class. All eyes were on her.

Could she do this? Then Lauren looked down at the sheet of paper in her shaking hands. She saw Ettie Shaw's handwriting and reminded herself of the hard lives her relatives of long ago had lived. It made her braver.

Lauren lifted her chin up and began ...

"Joe Shaw was my great-great-great-great grandfather!" said Lauren, hoping she'd got that right. "He got sent to Australia on a convict ship in 1836, for pickpocketing. He was the same age as us – twelve."

Lauren heard everyone gasp. She bet that her classmates pictured those criminals sent on the ships as grown men. Scary men, probably. Not young boys.

"Stealing is wrong," Lauren carried on. "But Joe and his little sister Ettie were homeless orphans. They must have been desperate for money. Lots of poor children lived on the streets in Victorian times in the UK. Joe was taken to Australia, leaving Ettie behind all on her own. She was just ten."

The boys and girls and even Miss Jenner were wide-eyed as they listened to Lauren.

"I know lots of people have relatives who were convicts," said Lauren. "But most people don't know much about them." She held up her sheet of paper. "My family is lucky – we've still got letters that Ettie sent to Joe when they were adults. This is a photocopy of one of them cos the real letters are so delicate. And I can't read it cos the handwriting is so fancy and complicated!"

Her classmates leaned forward to see the swirly, looping words on the copy of the letter.

"But here's what happened to them," said Lauren. "Joe was in prison for seven years for his crime. He worked with the prison guards' horses. When his time was up, he went to work on a cattle ranch."

"Like a cowboy!" Kenny shouted out.

"Yes, I think so," said Lauren. "Joe married the rancher's daughter and ended up having his own ranch in New South Wales. He lived till he was nearly eighty and had four children."

"What about his little sister? What happened to Ettie?" asked Bindi.

"There was some kind of fight when Joe got arrested, and Ettie was hurt," said Lauren. "It happened outside a shop that sold umbrellas."

A few children giggled. A shop that just sold umbrellas sounded sort of funny, especially in a country like Australia where it was so hot most of the year.

"Ettie was badly injured and the shopkeeper took her inside," Lauren carried on. "She stayed there in a room where the shop girls slept. When Ettie felt better, she told them she was good at sewing and they offered her a job making umbrellas and parasols and things."

"I'm so glad Ettie was safe," said Miss Jenner. "Did she work there all her life?"

"No," said Lauren with a shake of her head. "Ettie left when she got married. Her husband was a servant, but they moved to the country and opened their own shop. Their daughter became a headteacher, and their son was the mayor of his town!"

"Did Ettie and Joe ever visit each other?" Bindi asked.

"No, they never did," Lauren said. "It was too far and cost too much money in those days. But Ettie always ended her letters in a really nice way ..."

Lauren clutched the sheet tighter in her hand and told them the last line, which she knew by heart.

"Aren't we lucky, Joe? Till next time, your adoring sister Ettie."

"Well," said Miss Jenner. "That is very special, Lauren! What an amazing way to remember your heritage."

"And I have one *more* way, Miss," said Lauren with a smile. "My middle name!"

"Of course!" said Miss Jenner, clapping her hands together. "Well, thank you for your speech, Lauren Ettie Shaw! Can everyone give Lauren a round of applause?"

Lauren went back to her seat, and the sound of clapping rang in her ears.

She liked to think the applause was also for Ettie and Joe, who found their own way in the world and their own luck too ...

The facts behind the story ...

An important part of writing a book is doing the research, especially when it's a historical book. So I thought it would be fun to let readers know about the facts behind each chapter of the story. Maybe you're interested in doing your own research about the lives of Victorian children like Ettie and Joe!

CHAPTER 1

Mothers and children from poorer families often worked at home doing "piecework" while fathers went out to work. Examples of piecework included making fake flowers for bonnets and hats, putting matchboxes together, covering top hats in silk and stitching sacks.

The hours were very long, and the wages were very low.

CHAPTER 2

Diseases like cholera, measles, tuberculosis, scarlet fever, whooping cough, mumps and diphtheria were common in Victorian times and could easily kill. Babies and young children often died. Being rich didn't protect you against these diseases, but diseases spread faster in overcrowded, poorer areas of cities. Today, modern medicine and vaccination mean these illnesses are very rare in Britain, thankfully.

CHAPTER 3

Ettie's mother was killed by being slowly poisoned by arsenic, because she used it in her work. Arsenic powder made the emerald-green colour used in Victorian clothing, like the leaves in the fabric flowers. It was only later

in the nineteenth century that people realised
how dangerous arsenic was.

CHAPTER 4

Poor children sometimes tried begging or
street-sweeping to earn money. But some
attempted to entertain others for money!
They might turn somersaults, tell jokes or
sing songs for people passing by.

CHAPTER 5

There were no special clothes for rich people
or poor people. The poor just wore clothes
that had been worn by wealthy people and
mended and resold many times over. Some
tailors specialised in "translating" clothes,
which meant doing things like pulling apart an
old jacket and making caps out of the fabric.
Recycling was huge in Victorian times!

CHAPTER 6

I borrowed the character of Mr Fagin and his young gang of boys from the famous Charles Dickens' novel *Oliver Twist*. But it's believed that Charles Dickens used a real-life criminal called Ikey Solomons as the inspiration for Fagin. Solomons was written about in Victorian newspapers.

In *Oliver Twist* there is a young pickpocket called the Artful Dodger. It's likely that he was based on a real boy Dickens had read about called Samuel Holmes. Samuel was part of a child gang and was caught stealing some meat. He was transported to Australia at the age of thirteen and was imprisoned for fourteen years for his crime.

CHAPTER 7

Lots of children ended up living on the streets of cities, trying to survive. A slang word for these children was "guttersnipes". At the time of Ettie and Joe's story, the government was only just starting to consider laws that would protect children's well-being. It took decades for things to improve. In the meantime, street children were often scared of going to a workhouse as they had a bad reputation, working people very hard, with terrible food and conditions. Workhouses also split families up, with mothers and fathers, boys and girls all living separately. But for some children who lived alone, the workhouse could be their way out of poverty – the workhouse could train them so they could be employed as apprentices or servants when they were old enough.

CHAPTER 8

The well-being of animals was not considered important in Victorian times. But it was at this point that it became fashionable for people to keep pets. Poor people might keep a songbird in a cage at their window. Other popular pets were dogs, rabbits, parrots and monkeys – like the chained monkey dancing on the organ in this chapter. Cats were not a popular pet as people still thought of them as "working" animals, only kept for getting rid of mice and rats in shops and buildings.

In this chapter there's a mention of asparagus and watercress being sold from handcarts. To us nowadays they're not the most common of vegetables, but asparagus (known as "sparrow-grass" in Victorian times) and watercress were easily grown around London and were what poorer people would buy more often than potatoes and carrots!

CHAPTER 9

The fancy umbrella shop in the West End of London really existed and is still going strong today! You can search for James Smith & Sons online to see images of how very Victorian it looks – and you can picture Ettie and Joe outside.

CHAPTER 10

It was a difficult time for Aboriginal people when Australia celebrated its 200-year anniversary in 1988. These native Australians could trace their heritage back thousands of years – long before 1788. It's been common for many years to say that a country was "founded" when European settlers arrived in it. But these kinds of attitudes are changing, and the history and rights of native people around the world are being recognised more and more.

Our books are tested
for children and young people by
children and young people.

Thanks to everyone who consulted on
a manuscript for their time and effort in
helping us to make our books better
for our readers.